Mystery at Canyon Creek

Lisa Trumbauer

Reading Advantage Authors
Laura Robb
James F. Baumann
Carol J. Fuhler
Joan Kindig

Project Manager
Ellen Sternhell

Editor
Jeri Cipriano

Design and Production
Anthology

Illustration
Bill Petersen

Printed in the United States of America

International Standard Book Number-13: 978-0-669-51421-6

International Standard Book Number-10: 0-669-51421-7

4 5 6 7 8 9 10 - RRDC - 10 09 08 07 06

CONTENTS

CHAPTER 1

Nowhere-ville!

Mom and Dad were having problems, so I had to go to New Mexico. Needless to say, I was not thrilled with the idea. I mean, would you be? I'm a city kid—well, a suburban kid, at least. My cousins live on some sheep ranch all the way out in the middle of nowhere.

Nowhere, New Mexico, that is.

"You'll love it!" Mom had gushed at me when she told me the news. "There's plenty of room to run around and do things."

"What things?" I argued. "I had tons of plans with Davis this summer. Now you've gone and ruined them."

Mom looked at me with that penetrating gaze that drives me crazy, like she can read my mind. "Jared Pickett, you do not have 'tons of plans.' If this summer is anything like last summer, you and Davis will be looking around for things to do. Then you will be opening the refrigerator door every ten minutes and asking what we have to eat."

Mom had a point, but I wasn't going to retreat and surrender so easily. "This summer was going to be different," I told her.

"You're right, Jared," she said sternly. "It is going to be different. You're going to spend a month with your cousins Luke and Courtney in New Mexico. That's about as different from Philadelphia as you can get."

Then I said something I shouldn't have, something that sounds horrible the minute it leaves your lips. It was something I wished I could take back, but I couldn't.

"Yeah, and maybe when I come home, things will be different here, too."

I could practically see the words floating in the air between us. The words swirled above our heads until they dissolved into nothing but memory.

It took several seconds before Mom could answer. And when she did, she seemed tired. She seemed bone-screaming tired.

Mom sat down at the kitchen table and leaned her elbows on the green, padded tablecloth. She began to rub her forehead like she had a major headache or something—probably one that I helped create.

"Can't anything ever be easy?" she asked softly.

Then she raised her head, and I felt really bad for being such a whiner. I have never seen my parents cry, but I swear that Mom looked as though she could have burst out like a baby that minute. I felt like a complete baby myself for making her look that way.

I did the best I could to apologize. "Sorry, Mom. I didn't mean to make you mad. It's just that you and Dad are always fighting, and it's no fun around here anymore."

Mom could have said something snide. I know I would have. I would have said something like, "Then you should have more fun in New Mexico."

But she didn't say anything. Instead, she pulled out another kitchen chair and invited me to sit down next to her. I was almost afraid to take that seat. I was afraid that she was about to tell me something I didn't want to hear. Maybe Mom and Dad were getting divorced. I felt like covering my ears, but I figured that at thirteen, I should be brave enough to listen to whatever Mom had to say.

Mom took a big breath before she spoke.

"I know the past few months have been tough on you and Lizzie," Mom began.

Lizzie is my little sister. She's six.

"And you're right," Mom went on. "Dad and I have not been much fun to be around. But I think you're old enough to understand why."

She took another deep breath. "Money has been a little tight lately, that's all. And your dad and I seem to argue over every nickel either one of us spends. That's why I have been working so hard, trying to sell houses. And that's why Dad decided to go to night school, to get some extra knowledge to help with his job."

"Your dad and I need a month, just a month, to try to get things back to normal," she continued when I didn't say anything. "Summer is a good house-buying season. So I hope to have a lot of new homes to sell and clients to sell them to. And your father will finish up his evening class and begin taking on new responsibilities at work. Hopefully, that will lead to a raise. Does any of this make sense to you?"

I shrugged. I was kind of embarrassed that Mom was talking like this. I mean, I wanted to know what was going on, but at the same time, I didn't. Do you know what I mean?

All this time, I had thought school was complicated. It never occurred to me before that Mom and Dad had complications, too.

And this sounded so much more serious than my stupid problems. I mean, I had to deal with Dean Harber calling me "Jar of Pickles" and getting the entire seventh-grade class to do the same. (Get it? Jared Pickett—Jar of Pickles?)

I don't know why Mean Dean felt that I should receive his idea of a sense of humor. But for some reason, he had chosen me and singled me out to bully during P.E. and pick on at lunch.

It drove me nuts, but I didn't know how to solve my problem with him. For some reason, he didn't like me. Or he saw me as an easy target. I'm no wimp by anyone's standards, although I am still short, I guess. Dean Harber is a head taller than I am. Still, I usually stand up for myself. But Dean Harber had a way of getting under my skin and making me itch.

The only kid in school who hadn't taken to calling me Pickles was my best friend, Davis. We have been friends forever. Luckily, seventh grade was *not* forever. It was over now. And, hopefully, I wouldn't see much of Dean Harber in eighth grade.

Unfortunately, we would still be in the same middle school and I'd probably have to deal with him sooner or later.

Back to Mom. She was looking at me expectantly, hopefully. I knew I had to say something to make her feel better about sending me to New Mexico. I had to say something to show that I understood that Mom and Dad didn't mean this to be an exile, but more like an opportunity.

"I get it, Mom," I said. "You and Dad need to concentrate on work for a while, and you don't have time for me or Lizzie."

"Jared, we both work so we can afford to live in this nice house and have nice clothes and two cars to drive. I wish we didn't have to work so hard, but we do."

"Well, maybe I could watch Lizzie for you. That would help, wouldn't it?"

Mom smiled. "It would, Jared, and I appreciate the offer. But Lizzie's looking forward to spending time with your grandparents in New Jersey. I didn't think you would find staying with them that much fun. That's why I called my cousin in New Mexico. You met her kids once, remember? At my other cousin's wedding?"

I shrugged. "Sort of." I vaguely remembered them. Not many kids were at the wedding, so I kind of blocked out the whole wedding experience. I could see the outline of other kids in my mind, but I didn't remember anything specific about them.

Mom stood up, went into the living room, and came back with a photo album. She flipped a few pages, then she turned the book to face me.

"This here is my cousin, Elaine, with her husband, Dylan. You'll call them Aunt Elaine and Uncle Dylan."

"Okay," I said slowly.

She did some more flipping, then stopped again. "And here are Luke and Courtney, their kids. Luke is your age, and Courtney is a year or two younger."

I peered closely at the pictures on the page. I saw a boy with sandy brown hair, like mine. But that's about all we had in common. He was wearing corny cowboy clothes—a western-style shirt and neatly pressed jeans and even cowboy boots. He had his arm slung around a girl a little bit shorter than he. She was wearing an identical outfit, like they were twins or something. It all looked pretty hokey to me.

I could tell Mom was waiting for some kind of reaction, a positive one, I'm sure. "They look nice," I said lamely.

Mom smiled brilliantly. "You see? You'll have a great time in New Mexico. I know you will."

I'm glad she knew because I had no idea what to expect.

One week later, I found out.

CHAPTER

2

You're Not in Philly Anymore

"Freak!"

"Nerd!"

"Wimp!"

That was Luke and Courtney McGraw, my cousins, arguing as we played the Monopoly® game.

I had been in New Mexico for a few days, and I was beginning to get the hang of the place. The land was a bit more sprawling and open than back in Pennsylvania. The towns were less crowded than my own suburb. And the ranch had a lot more animals than I had seen in my entire life in one place.

When we turned into the drive of the ranch, we went under a wooden gateway kind of arch. The gateway had the name of the ranch, Canyon Creek. I couldn't see the house, but I did see something else—an animal with a very long neck.

"That's a llama," my cousin Courtney said. "Llamas help us look after our sheep."

"Along with Josie," Luke added.

"Josie?" I asked.

"Oh, you'll meet Josie," Luke said. "And look! There are the sheep!"

Now, I didn't see just one sheep or even a dozen or so. I saw what looked like hundreds of them! They grazed on the open land, a big, fluffy cloud at eye level. I had learned on the drive from the airport that the McGraws raised sheep for wool. Shearing season was soon approaching, so the sheep were especially woolly at this time of year.

Courtney even offered to let me help them shear the sheep. How thoughtful she was, hmm.

All kidding aside, I had decided after a few days that Luke and Courtney weren't all that bad. After all, it wasn't their fault that I had to go to New Mexico and stay with them for a month.

But do you know what? When I landed at the airport, they seemed just as nervous about my visit as I was about meeting them. At first, they kept asking me questions about life in the "big city." I have to admit that I played it up a bit. I told them how Davis and I roamed the streets late at night and hung out on street corners and went to all-night movies and stuff.

I totally made it all up. The reality is that Davis and I live in the suburbs. The closest we get to an all-nighter is when our parents let one of us stay the night at the other's house. Then we rent DVDs and stuff our faces with popcorn. And street corners? The corner of Forest Dale Drive and Green Briar Road isn't exactly a happening hotspot.

Still, Luke and Courtney hung on my every word. I used their awe of my "city ways" to my advantage, leading them to believe that I was tougher and cooler than I really am.

"Your life must be so exciting," Courtney had said that first night as we sat over a game of Monopoly and cups of hot chocolate. We were sprawled out across a thick, woven rug in front of a stone fireplace. The room was full of bookshelves and what I guessed was Native American art.

"Yeah, well, you know," I said, shrugging my shoulders casually.

"Albuquerque is the biggest city we have around here," Luke offered, "and it's not really all that big."

"Santa Fe's nice," Courtney said. "I like looking at all the art galleries and stuff."

Luke rolled his eyes at me. "Courtney thinks she's going to be an artist someday," he said.

Courtney lifted her chin. "So? What's wrong with that? It's better than wanting to be a professional mountain bike rider."

"Mountain bike rider?" I asked. This sounded cool.

Now it was Luke's turn to shrug. "Yeah, we have some really cool trails here at the ranch. And Dad's promised to take me to Arches to ride the rocks there. That's supposed to be the best in off-road riding."

"Arches? What's that—like, a bike park or something?" I really had no idea.

Luke and Courtney exchanged looks like I was a complete moron. At least they didn't laugh.

"Arches is a national park," Luke replied.

"Oh," was my brilliant reply.

"It's in Utah," Courtney explained.

Like that made any difference to me. New Mexico, Utah, Arizona—they all sounded the same, location-wise, at least. I know that in school we learned some things about the Southwest and the animals and Native Americans. But that's about all my brain seemed to have stored for future use.

Courtney must have noticed the blank look on my face. She jumped up from her seat on the floor and rushed to an overflowing bookcase. She came back with a large book and placed it on the Monopoly board.

"Hey! Watch it!" Luke said, trying to keep his houses and hotels on the right squares. He straightened out a few of the pieces.

"Who cares about this stupid game, anyway?" Courtney said. "You're already winning."

"That doesn't mean that Jared and I can't play," Luke shot back.

Courtney merely shook her head. In that instant, as she turned pages in the book, she reminded me of Mom showing me the photo album of her cousins.

"This is a map of the Southwest," Courtney said, very helpfully. "We're here, just south of Albuquerque." She began pointing to other places on the double page. "This here is Colorado, and next to that you have Utah. And below that you have Arizona. And where they meet is called the Four Corners."

I looked closely at the map, and I could see what she meant. The corner of each state joined in one spot.

"That's cool, I guess," I said.

She turned to another page. "This here is Utah, and all these green blocks are national parks. And there's Arches."

"Courtney, that's enough," Luke broke in. "Jared's going to think we're a bunch of nerds or something, studying maps."

"I like to look at maps," Courtney said. "What's wrong with that?"

"Geek," Luke said.

"Freak," Courtney volleyed back at him.

They were at it again.

As I watched, Luke grabbed for the atlas, and before I knew it, he and Courtney were having a tug-of-war. It wasn't mean or vicious or anything. It looked like they did this stuff all the time. Aunt Elaine and Uncle Dylan didn't even come in to see what the ruckus was about.

Okay, so outwardly, this "city" kid rolled his eyes at such juvenile behavior. Inwardly, though, I thought it was kind of funny to see them acting like such dweebs. It made me feel—oh, I don't know—more at home than I had when I had first arrived.

Suddenly, a black-and-white rocket launched itself in the midst of the Monopoly board, spewing money and playing cards and game pieces everywhere.

"Josie!" Luke said desperately. "You've ruined it!"

Courtney began laughing, finally having wrenched the atlas away from Luke. She stood in triumph and raised the atlas above her head in a victory pose. "Good dog, Josie! Good dog!"

I couldn't help cracking up. Luke was trying so hard to keep the game together, but it was useless. The whole board was messed up, beyond returning it to the way it was.

Josie, it turned out, was a Border collie that helped Luke and Courtney and their family round up the sheep at the ranch. She proceeded to jump between my cousins, her tongue lolling out one side of her mouth. Then for some reason, she focused on me, took one flying leap, and plopped into my lap, licking my face.

Maybe a "city" kid like me shouldn't take so quickly to a silly dog, but Josie was all right.

Anyway, it wasn't the dog that I was afraid of. It was the llama—and the horse.

CHAPTER

3

Spit On

First off, let me explain that I'm not really afraid of animals. I mean, Davis and I have caught our share of frogs and turtles at the creek behind our houses. And, of course, I'm used to squirrels and rabbits, those kinds of creatures.

However, those animals are small.

The animals at the ranch were big.

Okay, the sheep are probably about the size of a large dog. I'm used to dogs, even big ones. But the horses were big, and so was the llama. I just felt nervous around them.

"Buster knows you're afraid of him," Courtney said one morning as we observed the llama over a fence rail. "He can sense that you're nervous."

"If you're nervous, he thinks you're up to something," Luke explained. "Like, maybe you want to hurt the sheep. Llamas are very protective of their herds."

Like I needed Luke to tell me that? Every time I got even close to a sheep, Buster plodded on over and stared me down with his big, hairy eyeballs. It was enough to give me nightmares.

"Well, I don't know how to be less nervous around him," I said.

Just then, a big glob of something wet hit me on the side of my head. Luke and Courtney looked stunned. Then they suddenly burst out laughing.

"You got spit on!" Luke guffawed.

"Yeah, Jared!" Courtney said around a giggle as she tried to dig a tissue out of her pants pocket. "Buster spit on you."

She was right. I had llama saliva running down my head and into my shirt collar.

"This is totally gross!" I said as I reached for the tissue.

"It's okay, Jared," Luke said with a pat to my shoulder. "I'm sure Buster will warm up to you. Or you'll warm up to him."

"I've got it!" Courtney exclaimed. "I know how we can get Jared not to be afraid of Buster!"

"I'm not afraid," I said hotly. I tried not to sound offended, but I was. Not only had an animal mocked me, but I was a coward to boot. "He just makes me nervous, that's all."

"Whatever," Courtney said. "I think you should go for a horse ride. Once you're comfortable around horses, then maybe you'll like Buster more."

It didn't sound like the brightest idea to me. But the day was warm and dry, and it seemed to stretch before us for hours. Trying to get me to ride a horse gave us something to do.

So we went over to the stables, and Courtney and Luke introduced me to Thunder.

"Thunder's really gentle," Courtney assured me. "You should have no problem riding her."

Luke and Courtney saddled her up.

Then Luke bent down and made a step with his hands. "Just put your foot in here and your other foot in the stirrup," he instructed. "Then toss your other leg over the saddle."

Oh, sure. It sounded easy, but it was more difficult than it looked. After about the fifth try—and plenty more giggles from Luke and Courtney—I finally plopped myself into the saddle.

"I'm so high up," I commented. Thunder had looked huge when I was on the ground. Now that I was perched on her back, she seemed about as tall as a skyscraper.

"You'll get used to it," Courtney said while Josie yapped at her heels.

Luke and Courtney slowly led me out of the stable, pulling on Thunder's reins. When I realized that I wasn't about to fall out of the saddle and that Thunder wasn't about to bolt, I felt a little better.

"This isn't so bad," I said.

"See? There's nothing freaky about horses," Courtney remarked.

"Or llamas!" Luke said with a laugh.

And that's when my nightmare began. We're still not really sure what spooked Thunder. Maybe it was Josie prancing at her heels.

Maybe it was a fly buzzing in her ears. I wouldn't even be surprised if it had been Buster, shooting his hairy eyeball at Thunder—or a big wad of spit.

Whatever it was, Thunder suddenly took off, ripping the reins from Luke's hands.

"It's just a bad dream," I said to myself as Thunder galloped roughly across the open field. "It's a nightmare, that's all. And when I wake up, I'll be safe and sound in my bed back home."

But I was already awake, and Thunder was no closer to stopping than a moment before. I had no idea how to stop the darn animal, and I didn't know where Thunder was taking me. The wind whistled through my ears as the horse tore up the ground, her mane flapping in my face as I struggled to hold on to the reins.

I found myself hanging on for my life! The stupid horse refused to obey my commands—not that I knew exactly what commands to give her. Luke and Courtney had barely had a chance to tell me what to do when Thunder had taken off.

Nightmare, I'm telling you!

Then I saw it, up ahead, the thing that the horse was heading toward. It was the natural place—the stable!

I tried to breathe a sigh of relief, but I inhaled a huge hunk of Thunder's bristly, black mane instead. Thunder had run a huge loop around the field. I watched through teary eyes as the stable loomed up bigger and bigger before us. Thunder flew inside the darkened doorway, and perhaps her eyes needed to adjust to the dim light as mine did. Because the next thing I knew, Thunder stopped abruptly.

Too bad she hadn't given me any warning, because I didn't stop. I kept right on going, over her neck and through the dusty air.

I landed in a soft pile of hay at the back of a stall in the stable. I swear I must have flipped over about a gazillion times. I think the only thing that stopped my freefall was the stable's wooden wall. My feet thumped against it as I rolled over in mid-air, and my body hit the hay with a soft thud.

It took me a moment to regain my senses, and even longer for Luke and Courtney to make their way to the stable, which was a good thing. I didn't want them to see how freaked out I was. I tried to breathe deeply and clear the tears from my eyes as I sat up and rubbed my shoulder.

Not all parts of that pile of hay had been soft, after all.

"Whoa!" Luke exclaimed as he leaned over me. "That was awesome!"

"Yeah, Jared!" Courtney agreed as she ran up. "That's the bravest thing I've ever seen! No one ever rides Thunder that fast."

Now they tell me.

"Are you all right?" Courtney asked as she bent down to help me up.

"Yeah, yeah, I'm all right," I said, scootching away from Courtney's outstretched hand. She didn't notice, though, and she grabbed my arm and helped me to my feet.

As I brushed hay from my shirt and legs and arms, Josie jumped around my feet, as if checking to make sure I wasn't hurt. I patted her on the head, pleased that the dog seemed concerned.

That's more than I could say about my cousins. I had been concentrating so hard on clearing all the hay from my hair and pockets that I hadn't noticed them. They were doubled over laughing.

I placed my hands on my hips. "What's so funny, you guys?"

"Geez, Jared!" Luke said when he could catch his breath. "The next time you want to be a human torpedo, let us know!"

"Yeah!" Courtney said as she tried to control a giggle. "We'll get Thunder all warmed up for you."

I wanted to be mad and say something snooty, but I couldn't. It *was* funny. And now that it was over, I could appreciate what a stupid sight I must have been.

So I started laughing with them, and it felt good to laugh. It seemed that I had been mad at Mom and Dad and Dean Harber for weeks. And more recently, I had sort of been mad at Luke and Courtney. Now it all seemed so stupid.

I plopped back down in the hay and kept on laughing, really loud. Luke and Courtney joined me. Before I knew it, we were being total goofballs, throwing hay at each other and chasing Josie through the stable.

Finally, we collapsed in the spot where I had first landed unceremoniously after my ride with Thunder. We were a bit exhausted but also a bit closer. Josie lay down next to me, and I ran my hand through her black-and-white fur.

And that's when a board from the stable wall clunked me on the head. And behind the board, we found something that was about to affect the rest of our month.

CHAPTER

4

A Hole in the Wall

"Ow!" was my first reaction. After all, when something big and wooden slaps you on the head, your first instinct is to proclaim how much it hurts.

Luke and Courtney hid giggles behind their hands.

"Go ahead. Laugh at the city kid," I said. But I was laughing, too. That was my second reaction.

My third reaction was to look behind me. I wanted to see what had taken the liberty to clunk me on my head.

And that's when I saw it. No, not the board from the stable wall, but a rolled-up piece of paper, stuck inside the wall.

"What's that?" I asked, rubbing my head with one hand and pointing with the other.

"What's what?" Luke responded when he came up for air from laughing so hard. He peered around my shoulder and spied the paper. "That's weird. I don't remember anyone putting anything back here."

Luke crawled around me and plucked the paper from the hole in the wall. "It feels kind of old," he commented. "Like it might fall apart in my hands or something."

"Then be careful with it, you big doofus," Courtney said. "Let's find a table and unroll it."

Luke held the roll carefully in his hands and stood up. We followed. Then we walked around the stable until we found an old blanket chest. Very carefully, Luke placed the roll on the top. Even more carefully, he began to unroll it. The paper was very fragile. It was a yellowish color, and the corners and edges were ripped and worn.

I held my breath as Luke tried to hold the edges down. I was afraid the paper would crumble in his hands. Courtney got up suddenly. She returned with two rocks. She placed the rocks on the edges, so the paper would lie flat.

Why hadn't I thought of that?

Even with the rocks, the corners still curled in, as if the paper had been rolled up for a very long time. Together, we stared at the scribbles and dribbles of ink on the paper.

"What is it?" I asked. "Can you make it out?"

"It just looks like a giant spider web of lines and crisscrosses," Luke remarked.

"I know, it does," I added.

We were all silent for a moment, studying the mysterious drawing before us. Then Courtney inhaled a huge breath.

"I know what it is!" she gasped.

"Well?" Luke asked when she didn't enlighten us further.

Courtney hesitated. "I don't want you to think I'm being overly dramatic or anything."

"Yes?" Luke and I said together.

Courtney nibbled her lip, as if nervous.

"You promise you won't think I'm being silly?" she asked.

Luke rolled his eyes at me, like we were in this together. I kind of liked it. It made me feel like Luke and I were best buds, like Davis and me.

"No, Courtney, we won't think you're silly," Luke answered.

"Well," Courtney paused again.

"Courtney!" Luke shouted.

"All right!" She took a deep breath, as if she needed to get it all out at once before she lost her nerve. "I think it's a map," she said quickly.

We peered more closely at the lines. They still seemed like chicken scratch to me. (Not that I've actually *seen* chicken scratch. But my first-grade teacher always described my handwriting like that—as chicken scratch.)

Courtney wiggled her way in between us. "See this line here? And this line here? I think this is the front and side border of our ranch." She pointed to some more scratches. "And see this wavy line? I think this is the canyon that borders the far side of our property."

Luke squinted, as if trying to see what Courtney so obviously saw.

When his eyes opened wide, he looked at her admiringly. "Hey, sis! I think you're right!"

Well, I definitely couldn't decipher their property boundaries. If that is what they "saw," then I'd have to believe them. But the map held other doodads as well.

"What about these things?" I asked. I pointed to some drawings that looked a bit different than just random scribbles. One was a bunch of circles, one inside the other, like the ripples in a pond. The other looked like a giant, squashed bug with only four legs. Still another looked like a bunch of building blocks with a round circle in the middle. A fourth doodad resembled a wheel with spokes—and a bunch of dots in between the spokes.

"They look like symbols of some kind," Luke said.

Courtney tilted her head, as if looking at the symbols from a different angle. "I guess they could be rocks or something on the ranch. I don't recognize them, though. Do you, Luke?"

"Not at all. But then, I've never really explored the entire ranch. Mom and Dad have never taken us all the way to the farthest border."

"How big is the ranch?" I asked.

"I'm not really even sure," Luke answered. "I think I've heard that you can walk across it in a day."

A day! I could walk across my backyard at home in, like, a minute! I didn't want to give away how cool I thought it was that their property was so big, so I said a simple, "Oh."

Courtney continued to study the map as Luke and I contemplated how big the ranch was. Then Courtney gasped.

"What now?" Luke groaned.

"Think about it!" Courtney said, getting very excited. "People don't just draw maps with funny symbols and then hide them. The map must have been hidden for a reason."

"Like what?" Luke asked.

"Like, the person who drew the map didn't want anyone else to find it."

"And why not?" Luke continued, humoring her.

"Because maybe the map leads to something special," Courtney said. She paused dramatically.

"Maybe it's a treasure map."

CHAPTER

5

Day Trip

Luke didn't seem as impressed by Courtney's idea as she was.

Okay, I was impressed, I admit. It sounded pretty exciting to me. I mean, I had never found an old map before. Maybe it *did* lead to a treasure.

"Courtney," Luke said with the patience of an older brother, "that's in your imagination."

Courtney looked crushed. I felt bad for her, and she must have sensed it. She looked at me and her face brightened.

"What do you think, Jared?"

Hmm. How to answer this question. If I said I believed it was a treasure map, I might sound like a silly child to Luke. If I didn't support Courtney, it would show that I didn't trust her judgment.

I tried, as the saying goes, to "ride the fence" instead. I really worked hard not to take either side.

"Well," I began slowly, "let's list what we know. Number 1, you think it's a map of your ranch. Number 2, it was definitely hidden in the wall. And Number 3, it looks pretty old."

"So?" Luke puzzled, looking at me and then looking at the map.

"So," I continued, "I think it's possible the map could lead to something important."

"Like a treasure!" Courtney said with a clap.

"Maybe," I drawled out. "Or maybe just someone's house, or maybe even just a trail for the sheep or a field for them to graze in. Who knows?"

"Of course, there's only one way to find out, then," Luke said, turning away from the map and looking now at Courtney and me.

"Yes!" Courtney cheered.

"What?" I asked, although, of course, I knew the answer.

"We're going to have to follow the map and figure out where it leads," Luke said.

We were all silent for a moment, thinking of what we might find. Courtney, I was sure, was thinking of hidden treasure chests full of gold. Luke was probably trying not to think about treasure, but I'm sure he was having a hard time not doing so.

What was I thinking? Well, part of me was thinking of treasure. The other part of me was thinking about how much trouble we could get into—or how much trouble we could find.

So, according to the map, it would be a day's walk to the canyon. Had I ever walked an entire day in my life? I don't think so!

We weren't able to do anything about the map just then. Aunt Elaine began calling us to dinner from the back porch.

Luke quickly rolled up the map as Courtney and I looked for a place in the stable to stash it. When nothing better presented itself, we gently put the map back in the stable's wall and covered it with the fallen board.

"We have to come up with a plan," Courtney whispered as we hurried back to the main house.

"Why are you whispering?" Luke asked in a whisper only a little bit louder than hers.

"I don't know!" Courtney giggled.

However, we weren't able to talk about the map that night. Aunt Elaine and Uncle Dylan decided that we should all go in to Albuquerque to see a movie. And the next day was impossible, too. It was Sunday, and my aunt and uncle had planned an outing for all of us—a day trip to Bandelier National Monument.

Now, my idea of a national monument is a big, historic building or statue. We have lots of those in Philadelphia, such as Independence Hall and the Liberty Bell. I've even been to Washington, D. C., a few times. When I heard the word *monument*, I was thinking of the Washington Monument. You know—that big, tall, white, pencil-like building?

So I was thinking it would only take us a half-hour at the most to wander through or around the monument before heading back to the ranch.

But I was about to learn another difference between Pennsylvania and New Mexico.

No wonder Luke and Courtney had groaned.

First of all, the monument was not close to the ranch. It was about an hour north of Santa Fe, which is an hour north of Albuquerque. So that's two hours up and two hours back.

More importantly, though, is that Bandelier is not just one building. It's a park—a really, really BIG park. And it's full of hiking trails and trees and animals and other kinds of nature stuff. But the coolest thing about Bandelier is what we really came to see—the cliff dwellings.

In school, we had studied Native Americans and how a long time ago, they used to make their homes in the cliffs of the Southwest. But learning about them in a book and actually *seeing* the cliff dwellings were totally different experiences.

When we first began to walk along the trail, all I could see were holes in a cliff wall, very far away and very high up. They really just looked like big bat caves or something. But as we continued our walk, an entire village complex appeared before us.

It was really just a lot of low, square walls of stone. But the walls were all connected. If you can imagine a giant, round apartment building, with lots of little rooms, but with the top blown off, that's what it looked like.

We weren't allowed to walk inside the stone rooms, but we could peer over the low stone walls, and the trail led through the whole complex.

We continued walking, and the trail started to climb up toward the cliff wall. The village complex below us looked really cool the higher we climbed. You could see how round it was, and you could see all the little chambers.

At the top of the trail, though, were the coolest things—the cliff dwellings. And the holes were high up in the cliff walls, but not too high. The park had placed ladders at some of the holes, so you could climb the ladders and go inside.

Most of the caves were just dark holes inside the cliff. But the walls of some caves were actually pretty bright inside and you could see a lot.

Luke, Courtney, and I had a blast running from cave to cave, climbing the ladders, and taking pictures of each other. We were total nut jobs. Luckily, the park wasn't very crowded. I'm sure other visitors would not have enjoyed our nuttiness.

We continued along the trail, which gradually began to go back down. It still traveled along the cliff wall, and we came to a section called the "long house." The wall had small holes spaced exactly the same distance apart, like where poles were placed to hold a floor up. Caves were above these small holes, and you could just imagine a family of ancestral Pueblo living here, along with other families and friends.

We couldn't crawl inside these cliff dwellings because they were too high up and the park hadn't placed ladders in front of them. We could only gaze up at them and wonder about how cool it would have been to live there.

"Yeah, but we wouldn't have had any electricity," Luke said. "No electricity means no TV and no computers."

"I think I could do it," Courtney said.

"Oh, yeah? Well, how about plumbing?" Luke reminded her.

"Plumbing?"

"Yeah, you know, like the thing that helps you take a bath and wash up at the sink. The thing that lets you flush the toilet."

"The electricity thing might not be so bad," I said. "But I don't know about not having toilets."

"Maybe," Courtney conceded. "But I still think I'd like to try it. Maybe just for a week."

"You couldn't last a day," Luke said.

"Could too!"

"Not!"

"Too!"

"Not!"

I was getting used to Luke and Courtney's kidding around like this, so I wandered off a few steps on my own for a moment. I could still hear them arguing—or was that debating?—about who could survive the longest out here. But I was staring at the cliff wall and wondering a few things myself, too.

I was wondering what that scratchy thing was on the cliff wall. And why did it look so familiar? Then it hit me almost as hard as the board from the stable. The place where I had seen that scratchy doodle before was on our treasure map!

CHAPTER 6

Not Welcome Here

"Hey, guys! Take a look at this!"

Luke and Courtney stopped their verbal jabs with each other and came over to my section of the cliff wall.

"Look at those scratches, right there."

"Where?" Luke asked.

"There!" I said, turning his head myself.

I kept my hands on Luke's head until I felt his head begin to nod.

"Okay, I see them. So what?"

"Don't they look familiar to you?" I prodded.

Courtney leaned on my shoulder and stood on tiptoe to see what we had focused on. "Oh! That's the symbol from the map!" she said, indicating the swirly, circular shape.

"That's exactly what I thought," I said.

"Hey, Dad!" Luke called to Uncle Dylan. "What are these things?"

Uncle Dylan and Aunt Elaine strolled over. They had a small map and a guidebook that they had purchased from the visitors' center.

But Uncle Dylan didn't need to look up the area in the guidebook. "Those are *petroglyphs,*" he told us.

"What are petroglyphs?" I asked.

"Petroglyphs are symbols that the ancestral Pueblo people made on rocks and cliffs a long time ago," Aunt Elaine explained.

"You mean, like graffiti?" Luke asked.

"Kind of like that," his dad explained, "but not quite."

"The Native Americans drew these pictures to tell about themselves," said Aunt Elaine. "Each petroglyph has a meaning."

"What do these petroglyphs mean?" Courtney asked.

"I don't know what these say, exactly," said Uncle Dylan. "But we have books at home about petroglyphs. The books will help you decipher them. Do you want to copy them on something?"

"Yes!" Courtney said, the artist in her coming to life.

"No!" said Luke, just as strongly. "We don't have that much time here. We'll check them out when we get home."

Aunt Elaine and Uncle Dylan smiled as they walked off down the trail, leaving Luke and me with a pouting Courtney.

"We don't need to know what these pictographs are," Luke said. "We just need to know what the ones on the map mean."

"Petroglyphs," I corrected. "You said 'pictographs.' It's petroglyphs."

"Oh, right," Luke said. "Petroglyphs."

"But I wanted to draw them!" Courtney said, close to a whine.

"Courtney, what's more important?" Luke reasoned. "Spending time here drawing these petroglyphs, or going home to figure out the petroglyphs on the map?"

"I guess," she said with a mock sniffle.

"So stop being such a baby."

"Am not!"

"Are too!"

Here we go again.

We arrived back at the ranch much later than we had thought. We were all starving after Bandelier, so we stopped in Santa Fe for some dinner. What a cool place! It's not a city like I'm used to. It has no big skyscrapers or anything. The buildings are all only two or three stories tall. And many of them are very Spanish or adobe-looking. I saw lots of red chili peppers hanging in doorways and from lampposts. And we gazed in the windows at tons of paintings and woven blankets and stuff.

Courtney wanted to go into every art gallery we passed, but Aunt Elaine and Uncle Dylan were able to steer us to a restaurant first. The food was spicy but good, and we talked a lot about Bandelier and the Native Americans who had once lived there.

After a long day of hiking and an evening of walking and eating, we were pretty tired when we rolled through the Canyon Creek arch. It was also pretty late. Aunt Elaine and Uncle Dylan ushered us off to bed, and before we knew it, Luke and I were snoring away like mad.

The next morning, Courtney was already sprawled out on the floor of the family's den, looking through the books on petroglyphs. She had taken out a pad of yellow sticky notes, and I could see where she had flagged a bunch of pages already.

"Any luck?" I asked, eating some toast I had grabbed from the kitchen. Luke was right behind me.

"Tons!" Courtney greeted us. "I went out to the stable early this morning, right after the ranch hands left with their horses. I copied the petroglyphs from the map."

She said the word like an expert now.

"You got out the map?" Luke asked, his toast frozen halfway to his mouth.

Courtney waved her arm in the air as if to wipe away his astonishment. "Don't worry, Luke. No one saw me. And I was very careful not to rip the map. I even put it back inside the wall. No one will find it."

"No harm, no foul," I said to Luke as I finished my toast. I joined Courtney on the floor. "So, what did you find?"

I could practically feel the excitement bouncing off her. "See this swirly pattern?" She held up a drawing she had made. Then she turned to a page in a book. The petroglyph there matched the one she had drawn.

"This is actually the same symbol we saw on the wall at Bandelier. It's the symbol for migration. It means that the people who once lived there had moved on."

Luke joined us on the floor. "That would make sense, since the people who had lived at Bandelier eventually left."

"Why would it be on the map, though?" I questioned.

Courtney got really excited now. "I think maybe someone found an old cliff dwelling, like those at Bandelier! And that's why the symbol is on the map—to show us where the old caves are."

Luke looked skeptical, but he was agreeable to the idea, too. "What about this symbol—the one that looks like a wheel?"

Courtney turned to a flagged page.

"This is the symbol for *peyote* (pay OH tee). Peyote is a type of cactus. According to this book, peyote was sacred to the Native Americans. I think it means that whatever this map leads to is also sacred."

"That might be a stretch," Luke said, trying to keep us all grounded. I could tell, though, that he was warming up to the idea of a treasure hunt.

"How about this symbol, with the blocks and the circle?" I asked.

"That's actually the location of a *kiva*. Remember those from yesterday?"

"Those were the holes in the ground, right?" Luke said.

"Yep! Sometimes they were used for storage or for meeting places," Courtney shared with us. "Maybe the treasure is in a kiva!"

"If there is a treasure," Luke reminded her. "And what about this last symbol? The one that looks like a squashed bug?"

"That's the creepiest of all," Courtney said. She turned to a page and pointed to the picture. I don't know about Luke, but I know a shiver went down my back. We read the words together:

"Not welcome here."

CHAPTER 7

We're Off

"Isn't that squashed bug and its message cool?" Courtney said enthusiastically.

"I don't know if *cool* is exactly what I would call it," Luke said. "I think *creepy* is a better word."

"Don't you see?" Courtney insisted. "It means that whatever is there is important."

Courtney had a point. "Not welcome here" sounded like a warning to me. If someone was warning people to stay away, then whatever the map led to had to be important . . . or dangerous.

Now, a rational person would have said, "If we're not welcome, then we shouldn't go." But who said that kids on summer vacation are rational?

Looking back, I don't think it ever occurred to any of us to call off our plan to follow the map. Then again, we didn't actually think we would find anything.

Following the map gave us something to do. Sure, Luke and Courtney could have tried to teach me to ride a horse or how to identify individual sheep. Or maybe even how to shear those sheep. But searching for buried treasure sounds much more exciting, doesn't it?

The biggest problem that we faced was how to convince Aunt Elaine and Uncle Dylan to let us go off on our own across the ranch.

With a trusty canine companion and a borrowed cell phone, it wasn't that difficult at all. We told them that we wanted to go camping and that we would take Josie along for protection. We said we would take a cell phone, too.

At first, Aunt Elaine and Uncle Dylan didn't seem too keen on the idea. We assured them, though, that we would not stray from the property lines of the ranch. We told them we would call if there was an emergency. Hurray for cell phones!

In no time at all, we had packed our gear, grabbed the map from the stable, and headed off across the ranch. (I sound like an old pro, don't I? *Gear*. All I had done was stuff some clothes in my backpack, along with a few granola bars. Luke was the one who had helped me strap a sleeping bag to my backpack. And Aunt Elaine gave me a thermos of water.)

It wasn't even nine o'clock in the morning. But I already felt like I had lived an entire day. The day and the ranch—and all the possibilities—spread out before us.

We walked for about an hour in silence. We had been so excited and cautious when we left the stable with the map that talking hadn't seemed necessary. Now as we walked, I absorbed the scenery of my cousins' ranch. Looking over my shoulder, I noticed the main house and the stables growing smaller and smaller. When I could no longer see them, I got a sick feeling in my stomach.

The sensation reminded me of a time when I went fishing with my dad. We had taken a charter boat off the New Jersey coast, complete with a captain and mate. The boat went far out into the ocean, where a run of tuna was supposed to be.

I remember watching the shoreline fade into the distance until I couldn't see it anymore. All around me was the ocean, and nothing else. We were but a speck on the big, blue sea.

This was how I felt as I walked with my cousins across their ranch. All around me were acres and acres of ranchland with nothing to break up the horizon. The land was totally flat. I couldn't see hills or mountains or people or animals (except Josie) or trees.

In the suburbs, you always ran into things. There were always buildings or roads or mailboxes or streetlights or signs or trees or bikes or parked cars or something around. You couldn't get lost there. The suburbs have too many landmarks for you to lose your way.

But here, I had no idea where we were walking. It all looked the same to me. It looked like you could walk for days and days without seeing anything new.

After about an hour, I finally had to voice my concern. "Um, it's not like I don't trust you guys or anything, but . . . well, like, do you know where we're going?"

"Sure," Luke said confidently. "I've ridden my bike out here tons of times."

"Oh." I guess that should have made me feel better. "But . . . but *how* do you know?" I asked.

"See that cactus over there?" Luke pointed.

I squinted and thought I saw something that could be a short cactus plant. "I guess."

"That's how I know where I am," Luke said.

Was that supposed to answer all of my questions? Of course, it didn't. But I felt I would be too much of a dork if I kept pestering him about it.

We walked for a few more minutes in silence, and I couldn't take it anymore. "But it all looks the same to me!" I persisted.

Luke hoisted his backpack higher on his back. "That's because you're not used to it. Trust me. I know where we're going."

"It's okay, Jared," Courtney said, placing a hand on my arm, like she was Aunt Elaine or something. "Even though we haven't walked to the canyon before, we know where it is."

"And my dad drew us a map," Luke said.

"Can we look at it?" I requested.

Luke and Courtney stopped and stared at me blankly, like I was weird or demented.

"I mean, just to make sure," I added.

"We could compare it to the treasure map," Courtney said. "We weren't able to do that before."

"That's not a bad idea," Luke agreed.

So we plopped down on the ground. Josie wiggled between us, her tongue lolling out. I took my thermos from my backpack and filled the cap with water. After a sip, I gave the rest to Josie.

Luke, meanwhile, dug out the map his father had given him. He also produced a compass from a side pocket of his pack. Courtney unrolled her sleeping bag, where we had rolled up the treasure map. Now we used her sleeping bag as a makeshift table. We placed their father's map on the sleeping bag next to the treasure map.

I could see how the maps were similar. So we discussed for a few moments where we should go next. Luke consulted his compass, and Courtney rolled up the map inside her sleeping bag again.

The day progressed in this way. We would walk for a while and then stop to check where we were.

It seemed that we were getting closer, yet at the same time, not close enough. The canyon still seemed as far away to me as when we had started, and the day was more than half over.

Around five o'clock, we stopped once again to rest and read the maps. We were so intent on the maps, in fact, that we didn't pay any attention to the weather. That was silly. With so much land around us, we should have seen the dark clouds scurrying across the sky.

Now they were right on top of us, and they were sharing their rain with us!

"Yikes!" Courtney said, rolling rapidly to protect the map.

We stuffed all our things back into our backpacks and took off running. Josie yapped at our heels, thinking it was a game or a race. I didn't know where we were running to, but Luke seemed to be heading for something.

"There's an old shed not far from here!" he shouted above the rain. "We can stay there for a while."

So we jogged some more. Just when I thought I would collapse from exhaustion, I saw a bump in the distance.

"There it is!" Courtney exclaimed.

Even though I didn't think I had much energy left, the sight of the bump revived me. I took off in a rush, and I beat Courtney and Luke by at least fifteen seconds.

I think that was quite an accomplishment for a city kid like me, don't you?

We collapsed inside the cabin, dripping wet and totally wiped out. Josie wiggled and sprayed us with wet-dog water. Then she wandered around, sniffing in all the corners of the cabin.

The place wasn't much to look at. A table stood in the center of the wooden floor with nothing on it. An old cot with a wormy-looking mattress was against one wall, and an old desk sat along another. Two windows, bare of curtains, let in a little bit of light. A stove with a pot and teakettle rounded off the other wall. And that was it.

But do you know what?

It was awesome!

Little did we know that the cabin held another clue about the treasure at Canyon Creek.

CHAPTER

8

A Secret Hideout

After we stopped gasping for air on the floor, our first priority was getting dry. We all had packed a change of clothes in our waterproof backpacks. We just hadn't thought we would need them so soon. We all promised to turn our backs and quickly change, no peeking allowed. I guess they felt as awkward about changing out in the open as I did.

Finally, in dry clothes, we looked around for a place to hang our wet things. It was then that we started exploring the cabin more carefully.

It really was awesome. Okay, so it wasn't that big. It was more like a clubhouse or something. The roof went straight across the top, like a box, and you could see each individual wooden board. In fact, you could see the wooden boards that made up the walls and the floor, too.

It wasn't like a room at home, where the walls are smooth and glazed over. You could even see the nails that held the whole place together. It looked like something that maybe Davis and I would have built in my backyard.

"I like this place," I said to my cousins.

"It keeps the rain out," said Luke.

"I wonder what it was used for," Courtney said, wandering around and touching things.

"Dad and I stopped here once when we were riding mountain bikes. Dad said it's an old shepherd's shed. You know, like where the shepherds spent the night instead of going all the way back to the ranch."

"That would explain the cot," said Courtney.

"And the stove," I added. I was laying my wet clothes across the handles of the stove's oven door. It seemed like as good a place as any for my clothes to dry.

Courtney hung her clothes on the metal headboard of the cot. Then she picked up a broom and began to sweep.

"Why are you doing that?" Luke said, looking at her like she was from Mars.

"Because it's dirty," Courtney said reasonably. "And if I'm sleeping on the floor tonight, I don't want it to be in the middle of a dirty floor."

I didn't want to point out to her that if we slept outside, it would be in the dirt anyway.

"I guess we could stay here," Luke said.

"Sure, why not?" I said, getting into it. I grabbed a tattered rag from a peg on the wall and began wiping off the table. "We could pretend that this is our own secret hideout."

"Yeah!" said Courtney. "We're, like, Indiana Jones or something, and we're on an expedition to unearth a famous relic!"

"Or buried treasure!" I shouted.

"Or priceless jewels!" Courtney sang.

Now Luke included me in his "you're from Mars" look. "You guys have lost it."

"Come on, Luke. Don't be such a grouch," Courtney said, twirling around the floor with the broom.

Okay, so I was joining Courtney in her goofy ideas. Not too cool for a thirteen-year-old, I know. But when you're out in the middle of nowhere, in some rundown shack, it seemed kind of natural. The rain was pounding really hard against the wooden roof, and no parents were anywhere within shouting distance. We could do, or pretend to do, whatever we wanted.

I tried to get Luke into the spirit of things. I knew he wanted to, but he also wanted to act "mature" in front of his kid sister. I knew the feeling. So I held a corner of my rag in each hand, and I spun the rag around until it was nice and tight. Then I flipped one end and hit Luke on his rear.

"Hey! What did you do that for?" he yelled.

"If I'm Indy, then this is my whip."

"What does that have to do with hitting me?"

"Well, I thought I saw a big, hairy scorpion on you," I said with a totally straight face.

"What?" Luke shrieked. Then he jumped around for about fifteen seconds.

Then I gave him a look.

He realized that I was only kidding. "You dork!" he laughed.

"Right back at you," I said, flipping my rag-whip again. Courtney joined in and pretended that her broomstick was a sword. Luke grabbed the pot from the stove and pretended it was a shield. Before you knew it, we were totally clowning around, acting like the biggest bunch of nerds or something. And no adults were there to tell us to stop!

After our mock battle, Luke phoned home to tell his parents where we were. Then we set about making dinner. We decided not to try the stove. It could blow up, after all. But we did manage to start a small fire in a big frying pan that we set on the stove. We had brought some hot dogs with us, and we speared them on the ends of sticks we found outside. Then we roasted our dogs over the frying-pan fire. It was one of the best meals of my life.

Luke had even packed some popcorn in a tin pan covered with tinfoil. While Courtney and Luke argued about the best way to make all the kernels pop evenly, I sat down at the desk and waited.

Now, I know you're not supposed to rummage through other people's things. But I figured that whoever used the shed last didn't care about what was still there. Otherwise, he or she wouldn't have left anything behind, right?

So I opened some drawers. I didn't see much of anything until I spotted an old newspaper article stuck in the back of one of the drawers. I pulled it out and began to read, and what do you know? The article is all about a rancher named Vern Thornton and the mysterious treasure he apparently found.

"Hey, guys! Look at this!" I hollered over the sound of popping corn.

"Almost done, Jared, wait a sec," Luke said, fully concentrating on the tinfoil contraption of popcorn and the frying-pan fire. "This would have been a lot easier outside on the ground."

"But it's *raining* outside," Courtney said, hand on hips as she watched him.

I waited impatiently as the pops occurred less often and then finally stopped. Luke placed the tinfoil pan on the stove. Then he grabbed my rag-whip from the table. Wrapping it around the handle of the frying pan, he rushed to the door.

"Courtney, open the door!" he ordered.

"But we'll let in all the rain!" she said.

"Better the rain than we burn down the place!" Luke said urgently, fire crackling in the pan.

Courtney finally got the message. She rushed over and yanked open the door. Luke carefully set the frying pan on the ground, as far from the shack's wall as he could. He watched as the rain made the fire sizzle, then sputter out.

"Phew!" he said, slamming the door on the rain. "It's really raining out there."

"Did you see anything else outside?" I asked, suddenly petrified.

"No, why?"

I forgot the old newspaper clipping I held in my hand. Instead, my gaze was glued to one of the windows. Night was falling fast over the ranch, leaving but a trace of daylight left.

But it was enough light to see by.

And it was enough light to cast a shadow on the window. The shadow was of a tall figure peering inside.

CHAPTER

9

The Year of the Vern-Man

Courtney screamed.

It was an eerie sound in the old wooden shack. The scream echoed off the walls and mingled with the sound of the rain.

And it scared me nearly to pieces. Yet the figure outside the window was much scarier.

"This is just great!" Luke whispered sarcastically. "If whoever that is didn't know anyone was in here before, he does now."

"He would know anyway," Courtney whispered back fiercely. "We have light in here from the candles we lit, dummy."

"I'm not a dummy!" Luke hissed.

"Are too!" Courtney bantered back.

"Are not—"

"Guys!" I interrupted them. "I don't think this is the time for one of your arguments. We have a real problem here!"

Luke and Courtney blinked at me, like a couple of owls. "What should we do?" she asked.

"Why do we have to do anything?" Luke said seriously.

"We can't just pretend that someone isn't out there," I said. "Wait! Did you hear that?"

"What? What!" Courtney almost wailed. But she didn't. She kept it to a little whimper.

"There it is again! It's a shuffling sound," I told them.

"I hear it," Luke said.

Josie heard the sound, too. But she was strangely quiet at the moment.

"I hear it!" said Courtney. "What is it?"

I don't know where I found my nerve, but I did. Maybe it was because I had been staring at the shadow longer than Courtney and Luke had. The shadow was beginning to look like something very familiar to me.

A friendly bark and a tail wag from Josie confirmed my suspicions.

I walked purposely to the door and wrenched it open.

"Jared!" Courtney screamed. "Don't!"

And then the scary creature stuck its head through the door.

"Buster!" Luke sighed with relief.

Yes, our creepy shadow was none other than Buster the llama, the Spitting Wonder.

Buster leaned his long neck inside the cabin, as if checking everything out. Josie ran up to him and leaped up, as if happy to see the llama.

I did not feel the same. I moved away from the door and sat back down at the desk. "What is he doing here?" I asked.

"He must have followed us," Courtney said, reaching up and stroking his neck. "Eeuw! He's really wet and stinky. It's a good thing he's cute."

"Cute?" I thought. "On what planet?" Out loud, I said, "But why would Buster follow us?"

"He is probably protecting us," Courtney explained. "Remember how we told you that llamas are protective?"

"But then who's protecting the sheep?" I was totally baffled. I could see why a dog would follow a person or people, but a llama?

Luke shrugged in answer to my question. "I'm sure the sheep are fine."

"And now Buster can watch over us," Courtney gloated.

"Great. Maybe he can protect us by spitting on me," I groaned.

"Don't be silly," Courtney said, giving Buster a final pat. "Buster didn't spit on you when you opened the door. For the first time, you weren't afraid of him."

Hey, she was right. I hadn't thought of that.

Bowing out of the cabin door, Buster headed back outside. We could see him through the doorway, settling down beside the cabin.

"Will he be okay in the rain?" I asked. I wasn't up to speed on my llama know-how.

"Oh, sure," Luke said. "Don't worry."

"He sleeps outside with the sheep all the time," Courtney assured me.

Why I was worried about the stupid llama, I had no idea.

"Oh! I almost forgot!" I changed the subject and picked up the faded newspaper article. "I found this old newspaper clipping in the desk."

"What is it about?" Courtney asked. She opened the tinfoil pan of popcorn and brought it to the table, totally unafraid now.

"Listen, and let me know what you think," I said. Then I began to read. "'On Tuesday, April 22, miner Vern Thornton was finally found. He had been reported missing by his wife last month.'"

"A missing miner, huh?" Luke said through a mouthful of popcorn.

"Wait!" I said, then continued. "'When asked where Mr. Thornton had been, he claimed to have found a secret cave full of jewels.'"

"A cave!" Courtney gasped.

"'When officials asked Mr. Thornton the location of this cave, he declined to comment. He did, however, explain that he had drawn a map of the cave's location. Further interrogation revealed that Mr. Thornton hid the map for safekeeping.'"

"Do you think Thornton's map is our map?" Luke asked.

"I think it might be," I said. "Let's take a look at it."

We unrolled Courtney's sleeping bag and placed the map on the table. We searched the map for some identification.

"Does this look like the initials *VT*?" Luke asked, pointing to some scribbles.

"I thought that was a bird," Courtney said.

"How about this—is this the number fifteen?" I asked, pointing to a corner of the map.

"That could be a distance or something," Luke suggested.

I didn't think so. "Fifteen, fifteen," I said aloud. Then it occurred to me. I grabbed the news article and looked at the date. "April 23, 1915!"

"The number on the map is the year when Vern Thornton drew it!" Courtney exclaimed.

"And it's been hidden in the stable all this time," Luke said, awed.

It was an amazing revelation. The newspaper article confirmed what we had suspected and what we had secretly hoped for. The map *did* lead to some sort of treasure.

With visions of jewels and gold dancing through our heads, we moved the table to one side of the shack. Then we spread out our sleeping bags on the floor. We blew out the candles and tried to get some sleep.

But it was difficult to sleep. I was lying on one side of Luke, Courtney on his other side. I listened to the rain as it fell against the roof, and I thought I heard Buster snuffle outside. Josie curled up between Luke and me. With a sigh, she soon fell asleep.

When we had set out that morning, I thought I would be afraid to sleep alone out in the middle of nowhere. But that night, I never felt safer in my life.

The morning greeted us with brilliant sunshine and cheer.

"You'd never guess it had rained yesterday," I said with surprise from the doorway of the shack.

It was like the thirsty ground had sucked up all the water overnight. The land had been left awash in shades of reds, golds, and greens.

We quickly ate some granola bars and drank some water. Then we packed up all our stuff. With Buster now along, we loaded him with our supplies.

We took a quick look at both maps before we left, and Luke consulted his compass. Then we were off. Josie romped on ahead of us. Buster plodded along behind.

We reached the canyon by midday.

"The canyon marks the end of our property," Luke informed me. "It's what the ranch was named after—Canyon Creek."

It wasn't a very deep canyon, maybe like the end of a deep swimming pool. The other side was about the width of a two-lane road. A creek ran at the bottom of the canyon. The creek was a bit swollen from the rains the night before. But it wasn't too scary or intimidating. That is, until the edge of the canyon crumbled beneath my feet, and I went tumbling over the side.

CHAPTER 10

Lead the Way

I could hear my cousins shouting my name as I tumbled down into the canyon.

I didn't drop like a stone over a cliff. I was more like a bag of laundry that you might drop down the stairs on your way to the laundry room. I kind of somersaulted my way down, kicking up mud and dirt as I went.

It didn't take long for my somersaulting to stop. The canyon wasn't that deep. I lay sprawled out on my back, gazing up at the blue-blue sky overhead. I wondered what it was about New Mexico that had me falling all the time—first, off a horse and now, off a canyon. Geez!

"Jared!" Luke and Courtney called down to me. "Are you all right?"

I turned my head first left, then right. Then I tried moving my arms and legs. Everything seemed to be in working order. "Yeah, I think so," I yelled back.

A big, slobbery tongue licked my face.

"Josie!" I laughed. "I'm all right, really!"

She continued to lick me, barking in between swipes with her tongue.

"Okay, okay!" I said, trying to shoo her away. "I'll sit up and show you I'm okay."

And it was as I sat up that I noticed the canyon wall in front of me. The canyon wall was decorated with dozens of petroglyphs.

"Hey, guys!" I called up to my cousins. "Come on down here!"

"Do you need us to help you get back out?" Luke called out to me.

"No! I think I may have found something important!" I called back to him.

"Like what?" Courtney asked.

I was growing impatient. "If we keep shouting back and forth like this, we will be here all day," I called out again. "Just come on down and find out!"

I could hear Luke and Courtney arguing above me, but I tuned them out. I carefully got to my feet, making sure that no bones stuck out at weird angles. All was well.

The petroglyphs were on the wall across the creek, so I sloshed my way over. The creek wasn't very high, maybe about mid-shin. Josie followed, playing in the water and chasing sunbeams. Then, she stopped and took a few quick laps of water.

While I waited for my cousins to join me, I studied the old drawings. They were so cool! It was like a secret code or something. The canyon wall itself was the color you'd expect—brown. But the wall with the petroglyphs was black, and the petroglyphs were brown.

Does that make sense? It was like the petroglyphs were a negative, like you get when you have pictures developed.

The petroglyphs were totally different from the ones at Bandelier. Those had just been like carvings in the wall. These were actual drawings.

And the wall was covered with so many different ones! Some were animals, some were handprints, and some were squiggly lines that might represent snakes or water waves. There were also some people with triangular bodies. There was even a swirly, circular thing, like the migration symbol.

I was so absorbed with looking at the wall that I didn't hear Luke and Courtney when they came up behind me. Instead, the shadow of Buster's long neck and big head distorted my view.

"Guys, look at this!" I said, turning to my cousins. When they didn't say anything, I finally looked at them.

They were trying really hard not to laugh.

"Are you laughing at the city kid again?" I asked, but without any anger.

"Jared!" Courtney said. "You're covered with mud!"

I looked down at myself. "I guess I am. But look at these!"

Finally, they turned their attention from my muddied condition to the symbols on the wall.

"Whoa!" Luke exclaimed.

"Exactly!" I said.

"I think we are definitely in the right area," Courtney commented. "But which way should we go now?"

We had only two choices—left through the canyon or right. I felt that the petroglyphs probably held the answers. We had a fifty-fifty shot either way we chose to go.

Then I took a closer look at the people figures, and I noticed their feet. Both feet of each triangle person were pointing right. Perhaps these ancient art figures were pointing us in the right—I mean, correct—direction.

"What do you say we go right?" I suggested, indicating the figures on the wall.

"I like it!" said Courtney. "Let's go!"

So we followed the creek, walking down inside the canyon. The creek was on our right side, the canyon wall on our left. Every few feet we would see another little petroglyph person with its feet pointing to the right. Once again, Josie ran on ahead, and Buster brought up the rear.

We had walked for about half an hour when Josie stopped and began barking.

"What is it, Josie?" Luke called to his dog.

Josie just kept barking and wagging her tail, so we rushed over.

We stopped just as quickly as we had hurried.

Josie was standing before a huge hole in the ground. If we hadn't been watching where we were going, we would have toppled right in. One topple a day is enough for me, thank you.

"Oh!" Courtney said, as we peered over the side. "I know what this is!"

We watched as she unbuckled her sleeping bag from Buster's bundle. Unrolling it, she spread out the map and pointed to one of the symbols.

"Remember this one?" said Courtney. It was the symbol that looked like building blocks with a circle within it. "This is the symbol for a kiva. We saw kivas at Bandelier."

"That's right." I did remember. "Kivas were underground rooms."

"So this hole is probably an old kiva," Courtney continued. "And it's on the map. That means we're definitely going in the right direction!"

Her excitement was contagious. I felt my heart pounding hard with anticipation.

We were close—very close.

We carefully made our way around the kiva, then continued on. The little people figures continued as well, as if they were walking along with us.

Then the people figures changed. Instead of a person, we saw a giant, squashed bug. That was the symbol that meant "not welcome here."

Beside that symbol was a cave.

"What do you think?" I whispered. "Could this be it?"

"I don't know," Luke whispered back. "Why are we whispering?"

"I don't know!" I again whispered. And I really didn't! It just suddenly seemed like the thing to do.

"Should we go inside?" Courtney asked, also in a whisper.

The next voice we heard was definitely not a whisper.

It declared very loudly, "I don't think any of you are going anywhere."

CHAPTER

11

Carter's Quest

The voice was Carter's, one of the McGraws' ranch hands.

Carter was a tall and big man. His jeans were scuffed and dirty, and his T-shirt was a smudgy mess. He also had streaks of dirt across his face and arms, like maybe he had been walking in dirt. He held a rope in one hand and a gun in the other.

Of the two—the gun and the rope—I'd say the gun held our attention the most. "Carter!" Courtney cried. "What are you doing?"

"Why, I've been following you," Carter announced, an evil smile spreading across his face.

"Following us?" Luke swallowed. "Why?"

"Because of the treasure, of course," Carter answered. "That's the only reason I took the job on your family's stupid ranch—to find Vern Thornton's treasure."

"You know about the treasure and Vern?" Luke said, shocked.

"It amazes me how clueless you McGraws are. Vern Thornton was my great-great uncle."

I think we all gasped at this revelation.

"Surprised, huh?" Carter smirked. "The tale of Uncle Vern's treasure has been in my family for decades. Everyone believed it to be just that—a story—but not me. I've been searching for that treasure for years."

"Why do you think we know where it is?" I asked, trying to find some city courage somewhere.

Carter shuffled his feet. "I saw the little missy here with the map yesterday morning. She seemed real excited about something."

"I told you!" Luke said to Courtney.

"It's not my fault!" Courtney stuttered.

"Is too!"

"Not!"

"Guys!" I interrupted. Geez! "Go on, Carter."

"After little missy here put whatever it was back in the wall, I sneaked into the stable and took it out again. Boy, wasn't I surprised to see that it was the map that Uncle Vern supposedly talked about."

"So why didn't you just take it?" I asked.

"I didn't want to raise any suspicions. When I realized that you kids were going after the treasure yourselves, I thought I would tag along and let you do all the hard work."

"But we haven't found any treasure," Luke pointed out.

"Not yet," Carter informed us. "But it looks to me like you have found the right cave. It's a shame, though, that you won't be able to see the treasure for yourselves."

Not wanting to think about what Carter meant to do, I had another question.

"If you were following us, how did you get ahead of us?"

Carter chuckled, twisting his face into a weird expression. He looked more sinister and dangerous, if that's possible.

"I saw you go falling into the canyon," he said. "I've been exploring this here area for so many months. I knew of a place not far from where you went over. I figured I could get ahead of you and surprise you."

"Well, you did do that," Luke remarked. I could tell he was trying to keep his voice steady, but it wobbled just the same. It was only a little wobble, though, barely noticeable.

Luke cleared his throat to get rid of the wobble and then stood up tall. "I wonder why Josie didn't bark at you?"

"That's 'cause Josie and I have become good friends, haven't we, girl?" Carter reached down to pet the collie, but Josie seemed to sense that something was wrong. She growled slightly, baring her teeth.

Carter's face lost its smile and his eyebrows drew downward over his eyes. He looked extremely evil now, like a villain in a bad western movie.

But this was no movie.

And the gun was very real.

Carter aimed the gun downward at Josie. "Hold off your mutt, or else she'll get it between the eyes," he ordered.

Courtney grabbed Josie's collar and urged her to her side. I gave Courtney credit for not crying. Her lip was trembling, but she was holding up pretty well.

I think we all were. Carter had me terrified, but I wouldn't let him see it. Questions, I thought. Just keep talking and asking him questions.

"So, um, like, what actually happened to your Uncle Vern?"

"And how would Uncle Vern know to hide the map in the stable?" Luke threw in.

Carter began twitching his gun hand. "Uncle Vern was a miner. He scoured all the caves in this area, looking for gold. One day, he just disappeared. He was gone for almost a month."

"The newspaper article!" Courtney said.

Carter nodded. "I don't know what you kids have, but an old newspaper clipping has been in my family's scrapbook. It's what started the legend of the treasure."

"Do you know where Uncle Vern was when he was missing?" I questioned.

Carter shrugged, like it was of little importance. "Not sure. Some people think he was living with the Pueblo. They think that whatever treasure he found was theirs. That's why he wouldn't reveal where it was—or what it was."

"But what about the map? And the stable?" I persisted.

"Records indicate that my Uncle Vern was friends with the old ranch owner. Vern probably thought the stable was a safe place. After all, horses can't read." Carter chuckled at his own stupid joke, wildly waving his pistol.

"So what are you going to do?" I asked, trying to make my voice not come out shaky. I think I did all right, although I was definitely shaking on the inside.

"I think I'll just tie you all up and leave you here for the moment. Then I'll go explore this here cave and see what treasure old Vern left behind."

"My dad will fire you!" Luke stated boldly.

Carter chuckled again. "Like I care about that stupid job?" He began waving his pistol at us. "Now why don't you all come over here and let me put these here ropes around you."

We didn't budge.

I don't know if we didn't move because we didn't want to obey him, or because we couldn't. We were too terrified.

Carter shrugged. "Fine. We'll do this the hard way." And he began moving toward us.

Just then, Josie jumped up and sank her teeth into Carter's arm. Carter swore viciously, shaking his arm and throwing Josie off. She hit the cliff wall with a nasty thud. Then she fell to the ground, motionless.

Courtney let out a startled cry and ran to Josie's side. Luke joined her, and I could see Josie's head lift slightly and her tail give half a wag.

Something inside me snapped. I turned from Josie and Luke and Courtney and faced Carter, but I didn't see Carter anymore. Instead, Carter's face became Dean Harber's, my own nemesis and enemy from middle school.

I couldn't take it anymore. Carter was just another type of bully, another version of one.

I'd had enough of bullies. I fisted my hands at my sides, ready to strike if he reached for me. "You're not going to do anything, Carter," I said.

"Oh, no?" he snarled. "And what makes you say that?"

"Because you're just a bully. And deep down, bullies are just cowards."

"Coward, huh?" Carter spit out. "Let's see how much of a coward I am when I walk away with the treasure."

"I won't let you anywhere near that treasure," I told him.

Now he laughed, loud and big. "And how are you going to stop me, little man? I'm the one with the gun."

Out of the corner of my eye, I saw Luke and Courtney, and Josie, too, get to their feet. "Well, I have something better than a gun," I informed him coolly.

"And what might that be?"

"I have a llama."

I turned around quickly and ducked behind Buster, just as Buster let loose with a huge wad of spit.

Bull's-eye! Or should I say Carter's eye? It was enough of a distraction to confuse Carter.

I saw Luke and Courtney duck into the cave, pulling Josie with them. I took off the way we had come, hoping that Carter would come after me instead of venturing into the cave.

I glanced over my shoulder and saw Carter stumble around behind Buster. He dodged Buster's head and long neck as the llama tried to batter him. Buster almost had him.

But Carter was more interested in me.

I put every ounce of energy I had into my legs, and then some. I was pounding on that dirt trail, staying close to the wall, knowing the place I wanted to stop—at the far opposite end of the kiva. I was hoping that Carter wouldn't notice my aimless running as I scooted around the kiva's edge.

I reached the opposite side just when I thought my lungs and legs would give out. Panting, I watched Carter come charging at me, not paying any attention to the ground beneath his feet. His piercing, evil eyes were aimed straight at me.

And then they were aimed straight at the ground below him. I saw a mild look of shock when he realized that nothing but air was beneath him. Then he fell heavily into the kiva below.

I peered over the edge and heaved a sigh of relief. The fall had knocked Carter temporarily unconscious. He wasn't so big and bad now. And he wasn't going anywhere for the moment.

Now there was one more thing I had to do.

I searched the area around me until I found what I needed—a long stick. Dipping the stick into the kiva, I speared it through the loops of the rope and hauled the rope up. I did the same with the gun, but it was a bit trickier to handle. The trigger hole was not as big or as flexible as the rope. It took some maneuvering, but eventually I got it.

I had never handled a gun before, and I didn't feel comfortable doing so now. Instead, I lifted a rock and stashed the gun underneath. Then I put the rock back in place. I figured someone could get the gun later.

Carter was still out cold, and I didn't think he would be able to hurt anyone anytime soon. I scooted back around the kiva and walked quickly back to the cave. Buster met me halfway, and was I glad to see him. I even gave his neck a big hug.

So there I was in the middle of the canyon, hugging a llama with hairy eyeballs. I was trying not to be a big wimp and blubber all over his furry neck. Then I heard Luke and Courtney hollering for me, deep inside the cave.

CHAPTER 12
Strange and Stranger

I grabbed one of the straps that held all our gear on Buster's back, and I pulled Buster inside the cave with me. I wasn't about to leave the llama behind.

The cave was dark, but small streams of light came in from holes in the wall and from high up above. I followed the light and my cousins' voices.

A sharp bark from Josie made me smile.

I remembered that we had packed flashlights, and I stopped for a moment to fish one out. Turning it on, I pointed it toward the floor. The beam helped me see the cave's narrow, tunnel-like passage. I quickly made my way through the tunnel as Luke and Courtney's excited voices became louder.

The tunnel stopped abruptly and opened into a much larger cavern. The ceiling was very high, maybe about forty feet up. Several holes let in lots of light.

But the holes weren't what made the tunnel bright.

It was the prisms of gems sprouting from rocks in the cavern's walls that made the room appear to glow so brightly.

"Isn't it amazing?" Courtney proclaimed with awe and wonder.

"What is it?" I asked, dumbfounded by the magnificence of the cavern's walls. It was like a kaleidoscope of colors and light and shininess. Soft pinks, light purples, deep golds, and brilliant greens all protruded from the cave's walls.

"It's the treasure," Luke said reverently as he waved his hand around the whole cave.

Luke was right. It wasn't a treasure that you would expect to find in a treasure chest. There weren't crowns of gold and pearl necklaces and diamond rings. Instead, we had found a cave full of rare rock formations of incredible colors and sizes!

"I wonder why no one has ever found this cave before?" Courtney puzzled. She reached out a hand to touch one of the gems on the cave's surface. "It's so smooth!"

"Maybe long ago, people obeyed the petroglyph that the ancient people had left behind: not welcome here," I speculated.

"And then the cave was forgotten over time," Luke added.

"And then Vern Thornton found it," Courtney reminded us.

"But he must have decided to keep it a secret," Luke said.

"So what should we do?" I wondered.

We all looked at each other. I didn't know what my cousins thought, but I was torn. Part of me thought it would be cool to remove some gems and take them with us. But then we would be as bad as Carter. The other part of me thought that the cave should remain a secret. But that would be a waste.

I think we all arrived at the same conclusion at the same time, but Luke voiced it first.

"I think we should call my dad," he said.

"Yeah," I agreed.

Courtney merely nodded. She seemed too overwhelmed to speak.

Luke rummaged around inside the packs on Buster's back until he came up with the cell phone and another flashlight.

"This will probably work better outside," he said. "Do you guys want to wait in here?"

"No, we'll come with you," I said. We had been together this long; we might as well all see it through to the end.

We all exited the cave, and Luke called Uncle Dylan. Then Luke, Courtney, Josie, and I sat around outside the cave and waited. Buster stood guard over us.

We talked a lot while we sat there, leaning against the cliff. I finally got to tell Luke and Courtney how I had led Carter into the kiva, and how I had been able to take away the rope and his gun. They told me how Josie had been only stunned by her collision with the wall, and that she seemed fine. Josie barked when she heard her name spoken.

It was strange, but as we waited for Uncle Dylan, we were both happy and sad. We were very excited that we had found the cave. We were proud that we were able to solve the mystery of the map and Canyon Creek. We were thrilled that we had bested Carter and saved the treasure.

Yet an underlying sadness punctured our happy mood. Perhaps we were sad because our adventure was over. Maybe it was because once Uncle Dylan arrived, the treasure would belong to everyone and not just to us or to Uncle Vern or to the Native Americans who had once lived there.

There was no way that such a discovery could remain a secret, and we didn't think it should. The cave and the precious gems inside were too beautiful to remain in the dark. They should be viewed and shared by everyone. A little corny, huh?

It didn't take long for Uncle Dylan to arrive. He had raced over in a SUV, and we showed him the cavern. He had brought along a camera.

Uncle Dylan took lots of pictures. He explained that in order to get the scientists or the geologists to come out here, he should have some proof. And he didn't want to carve into the wall to bring out a sample. He would leave that to the experts.

We also led Uncle Dylan to Carter. By the time we got to him, Carter was awake and very grouchy. He claimed that we had attacked him, if you can believe it. I showed Uncle Dylan where I had put Carter's gun, and that shut Carter up. Before long, the police arrived and took Carter away.

For the next few days, Luke and Courtney and I became minor celebrities. Lots of newspapers wanted to interview us and print our story. We tried to be modest about it, but it was all pretty exciting. Even Josie and Buster got their pictures in the paper. (I cut out each one of those articles and brought them back to Philly with me.)

And then, all too soon, my vacation was over. It was time for me to leave New Mexico. It felt strange to say goodbye to my cousins because now we had become more than just distant relatives.

We had become friends.

Courtney hugged me really tight at the airport, tears glistening in her eyes. Luke and I didn't know what to do. After all, we're guys. Guys don't hug guys. So Luke said something goofy to me about trying not to be too much of a city kid now that I was leaving. And I told him not to let Buster spit on anyone.

I invited them both to come visit me in Philly. We promised each other that we would keep in touch so we could plan for them to visit me.

The plane took off, and within several hours, I was home. And that felt even stranger. Or maybe I was the stranger. Things were better at home. But I felt different, like I was a different person than when I had left.

Well, maybe I was.

You know what? In September, when school started, Dean Harber didn't bother me anymore. Maybe it was because I was now taller than he was. (The New Mexico air must be good for growing things!) Or maybe it was because I couldn't be bullied anymore.

After all, if I could stand up to spitting llamas and runaway horses and crumbling canyons and gun-toting ranch hands, Dean Harber was nothing.

And that *was* something.